CH00840537

RUPERT™

and the Tree House

by Alison Green
Illustrated by Marjorie Owens

Methuen Children's Books

"At last!" sighed Mr Bear, hammering in a nail. "I thought we'd never get this shed finished. Now let's just clear up those spare planks and then I'll be ready for a cup of tea."

"Could *I* have the planks, please, Dad?" asked Rupert.

"Yes, of course," said Mr Bear. "Haven't you had enough of building for one day?"

"I'm going to build something that's much more fun than a shed!" laughed Rupert. "I'll just go and find Bill and Algy."

Rupert found his pals, Bill Badger and Algy Pug, playing football on Nutwood Common. "Hello!" he called, running over and tackling Bill.

"Oh, Rupert!" shouted Bill. "You've spoilt my goal!"

"Forget football, Bill," said Rupert. "I've had a better idea."

"What could be better than football?" objected Bill.

Rupert told his friends about the spare planks. "Why don't we build a tree house?" he said.

"Oh, yes!" chorused the others, and they raced back to Rupert's house to collect the wood.

Mr Bear gave the pals a long piece of rope to help lash the planks together and Mrs Bear packed a picnic for them. Soon they were on their way to Nutwood Forest.

"Do we really need the football, Bill?" asked Algy.

"Of course!" said Bill. "Once we've finished the tree house I can take my revenge on Rupert for ruining my goal!"

In the forest, Algy ran up to a sturdy old oak. "Let's use this tree!" he called.

"Oh no you don't!" snarled an angry voice above them.

"It's Raggety!" cried Rupert. The little wood troll scuttled to the ground. "Don't worry, Raggety," said Rupert. "We won't disturb you. We'll use this tree instead."

"I'm going to climb up really high!" shouted Bill. "Bet you can't catch me!"

"I'm not even going to try!" laughed Rupert. "It's much better down here. Come on, Algy, pass those planks up."

Algy passed three planks up, which Rupert wedged in the branches to make the floor of the tree house.

Algy had just climbed up to join Rupert when a strange
drumming noise broke out above them.

"What are you doing, Bill?" called Rupert.

"Nothing," said Bill. "The noise is coming from the other
side of the tree. I'll just swing round and see what it - Ow! -
Oh, no! He-e-e-l-p!"

There was a crash and Bill came tumbling down through the
branches. He hit the edge of the planks and all three pals were
catapulted to the ground.

"What on earth . . . ?" began Algy.

"Sorry!" gasped Bill. "There are woodpeckers up there. One
of them just attacked me!"

"But it's not like woodpeckers to attack anyone!" said
Rupert. "They are my friends. What could have happened?"

"I don't know," said Bill, "And I'm not going back up
there to find out!"

"No," agreed Rupert, sadly. "We'd better leave them alone.
Let's go home."

At home, Rupert told Mrs Bear about the woodpeckers.
   "What could have made them so angry?" he asked her.
   "I don't know," she replied. "Why don't you ask the Wise
Owl to go and talk to them? But ask him nicely, won't you?
He doesn't normally wake up for another couple of hours!"
   Rupert ran to the Owl's tree and called softly up to him.

The Owl was rather cross and sleepy at first. "Who's there?"
he snapped. "It can't be time to wake up. It isn't dark yet!"

But when Rupert told him what had happened he became
very interested.

"Don't you worry, Rupert," he said. "Run along back home
and wait while I go and talk to the woodpeckers."

Some time later the Owl swooped down into Rupert's
garden. He looked very worried.

"I'm not surprised the woodpeckers are so jumpy," he said.
"They say there's a thief in the woods, going around stealing
eggs. The warblers have had three stolen, the nuthatches
have lost two of theirs.

"The thrushes and blackbirds have lost more than they can count and the poor woodpeckers are scared stiff that they'll be next. They moved their nest higher up the tree, hoping they wouldn't be found and couldn't believe it when Bill appeared right next to their new hole."

"But *I'd* never steal birds' eggs!" protested Bill.

"Of course not," said Rupert. "But they must be so frightened. They couldn't take any risks. I wonder what we can do? Let's all meet in the Forest and work out a plan. Mr Owl, could you fly on ahead and tell the woodpeckers not to worry any more? *We'll* help them catch their thief!"

"Of course," said the Owl. "I'll go at once."

When the pals arrived, Raggety ran up to them excitedly.

"*I'm* going to catch the thief!" he announced proudly.

"He's going to hide in the branches," explained the Owl, "right next to the nest. He'll blend in with the background so the thief won't notice him. If he sees anything suspicious, he'll raise the alarm."

"Brilliant!" said Rupert. "We three had better go down to the Common, otherwise the thief won't show up at all. We'll be close enough for you to call us if there's trouble."

Bill seized the football and raced off.

"Right!" he called. "I'm going to score a goal this time, and Rupert's *not* going to stop me!"

Bill sprinted away with Rupert at his heels and was just
heading for the goal when Rupert gave a loud yell.

"Oh, Rupert!" wailed Bill, as his shot went wide of the
goal. "You put me off again! Why did you screech like that?"

He turned round to look at his friend – and burst out
laughing.

Raggety had leapt onto Rupert's back and was gripping his ears with his sharp little hands.

"I thought I'd *never* catch your attention," complained the troll in his crotchety voice. "I called you, but you were too busy with your football. Come quickly! The thief has stolen one of the woodpeckers' eggs. The Owl is following him."

They ran back to the Forest and found the woodpeckers
looking very distressed. "We couldn't stop him," they said.
"He lashed out at us with a stick. We didn't stand a chance."

Just then the Owl swooped down. "I've found out where
the thief lives!" he announced. "If we hurry, we might still be
able to rescue that egg. Follow me, everyone!"

The Owl led the pals and the birds to the top of a hill.

"That's the place," he said, pointing to a solitary cottage.

"Right!" said Rupert. "Bill and I had better go down there while Algy fetches P.C. Growler. Mr Owl, could you and the other birds fly ahead and distract the thief?"

"We'd be delighted to!" said the Owl, and they sped away.

Bill and Rupert arrived at the house in time to hear a
commotion start up in the back garden.

"Hey! Get off my lettuces!" shouted an angry voice.

Bill giggled. "Good old birds! They'll keep him busy for a
while." The pals sneaked through the door and into a room
lined with glass cases full of neatly labelled birds' eggs.

There were chests of drawers, too, all filled with eggs.

"Gosh!" gasped Bill. "They're beautiful."

"Yes," said Rupert. "But they would have been even more beautiful if they had been allowed to hatch. What use are they like this? Think of all the poor birds who lost their eggs just so that he could keep them in a drawer!"

"Look!" whispered Bill. "There's the woodpeckers' egg."

Rupert picked it up. "It's still warm!" he said. "Let's go!"
He wrapped it carefully in his scarf and they crept outside.
But as they tip-toed up the path, the man saw them.

"Come back here, you little thief!" he snarled, grabbing
Rupert's arm.

"*You're* the thief!" said Rupert. "This egg belongs to the woodpeckers."

But as the man went to grab it back, the Owl swooped down and snatched his watch-chain from his pocket.

"Give that back!" shouted the man, letting go of Rupert's arm. "You're an even worse thief than this bear!"

"But you're the worst thief of all!" barked a stern voice.

It was P.C. Growler! "Good work, Rupert!" he said. "Now if you'll take that egg back to its owners I'll have a little chat with this gentleman down at the police-station. Give him his watch back, now, Mr Owl. I don't want to have to arrest you, too!"

The woodpeckers were overjoyed to have their egg back.
Rupert climbed up the tree and placed it gently back in their
nest next to the other four.

  "Now we'd all like to do something for you in return," said
the mother woodpecker. "If you three can put those planks
back where they were before, we'll do the rest!"

The planks were put back in no time. Then the pals sat
back and watched in amazement as all the birds in the
forest fluttered back and forth bringing twigs and leaves.

"What are you doing?" asked Bill, but the birds were too
busy to answer. They just carried on swooping and diving
and weaving twigs together until their task was complete.

The pals could scarcely believe their eyes. The birds had
built the most perfect tree house they had ever seen.

"It's wonderful!" gasped Rupert. "Thank you, everyone!"

"Watch me!" shouted Bill, climbing up past the roof of the
tree-house. "I'm going to be king of the castle!"

"Careful you don't fall again!" teased Rupert.

"I won't!" laughed Bill. "As long as no one attacks me!"

At that moment, they heard a tapping sound coming from just above Bill's head. "Oh, no!" cried Bill. "Not again!"

"Are there other woodpeckers up there?" asked Rupert.

"There might be," said the mother woodpecker, mysteriously. "Shall we have a look?"

The birds fluttered up to their nest while the pals scrambled after them.

"You look first, Rupert," said the father woodpecker.

Rupert peered in. "Oh!" he gasped. "Look, everyone!"

Where before there had been five white eggs, there were now five tiny, new-born woodpeckers!

First published in Great Britain in 1993
by Methuen Children's Books
an imprint of Reed Children's Books
Michelin House, 81 Fulham Road, London SW3 6RB
and Auckland, Melbourne, Singapore and Toronto
Text copyright © 1993 Reed International Books Limited
Illustrations by Marjorie Owens
copyright © 1993 Reed International Books Limited
Rupert Characters ™ & © 1993 Express Newspapers plc
Licensed by Nelvana Marketing Inc.,
U.K. representatives: Abbey Home Entertainment Licensing

ISBN 0 416 18786 2

Printed in Great Britain